To Jean with much love
V.F.
To my parents with love
T.M.

The publishers would like to thank
Michael Pollock of the Royal Horticultural Society
for his help and advice.

First published 1994
by Walker Books Ltd, 87 Vauxhall Walk
London SE11 5HJ

2   4   6   8   10   9   7   5   3   1

Text © 1994 Vivian French
Illustrations © 1994 Terry Milne

This book has been typeset in Stempel Schneidler.

Printed in Italy

British Library Cataloguing in Publication Data
A catalogue record for this book is
available from the British Library.

ISBN 0-7445-2803-8

The Apple Trees

Written by
Vivian French

Illustrated by
Terry Milne

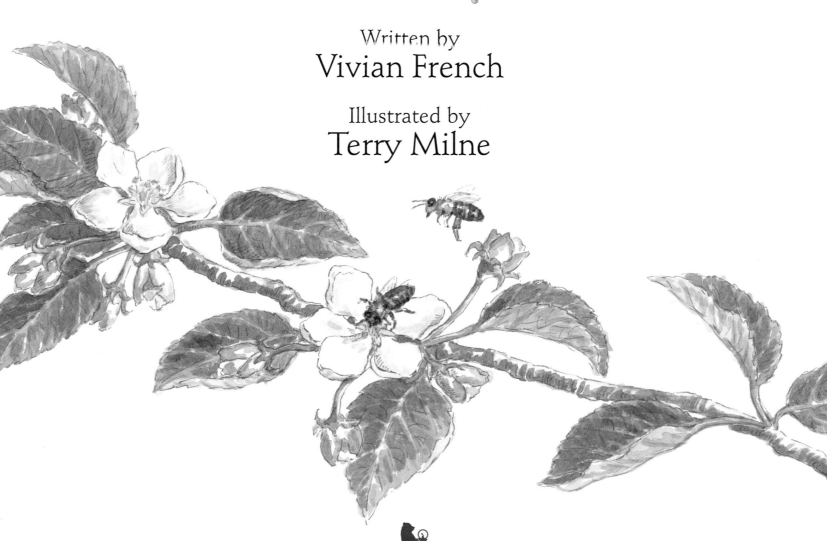

WALKER BOOKS
LONDON

We moved into our house in the autumn.
My daughter ran out into the garden
and looked all around.

"We've got a tree," she said. "What sort is it?"

The tree was leaning towards the hedge.

"It's an apple tree," I said.
"It looks as if it's very old."

Nan jumped up and down.

"I like apples. When will they come?"

"Next summer," I said.

7

SPRING

SUMMER

In the spring the tree was covered in blossom, and at the end of the summer we had baskets and baskets of big greenish yellow apples. We baked them and stewed them and made them into every kind of apple pie and pudding.

AUTUMN   WINTER

It was the same the year after, but the year after
that was different. There were only just enough
apples for two small pies.

"Maybe it wants company," Nan said.

We bought the little apple tree in the middle
of winter. Nan bent down and peered at it.

"Look," she said. "This one's a different
colour. Sort of greenish brown."

It made me think of brown silk stretched over
green, so that the green just glimmered through.
Nan put out her hand and touched the trunk.

"It feels quite smooth," she said. With
her other hand she felt the big apple tree's
rough flaky bark.

"Big and little," she said. "Old and new."

A NEWLY PLANTED
APPLE TREE NEEDS TO BE
WELL FED AND WATERED.

When the weather
grew warmer we planted
the little apple tree.
"It'll like having room
to stretch out," Nan said.

We watched our two trees all through the
last weeks of winter and the first days of spring.
One day Nan went out and came flying
back inside.

"I can see green! There's green
on the little apple tree!"

And there was. Tightly furled leaves
were pushing strongly upwards on the
end of every twig.

When the leaves opened
out, we saw that there were five
tiny clenched-up flower buds in
the middle of each cluster.

"Apple trees like the number
five," Nan said.

The big apple tree had hardly any leaves.
Its leaf buds hadn't really opened, and they felt
empty and brittle. The few leaves there were
looked dry and curly.

BEES AND OTHER
INSECTS CARRY POLLEN
FROM THE BLOSSOMS
OF ONE APPLE TREE
TO ANOTHER.

A week later the little apple tree was an
explosion of white and pale pink and darker
rose pink and gold and pale silky green and
darker green. Its satin-brown twigs
and branches were shining in the
sunlight, and bees were humming
and buzzing about
its flowers.

The big apple tree
was grey and bare.

When there were no flowers left on the little tree, Nan was sad. "It only took two months for all the flowers to come and go," she said.

We went to look at the big apple tree.

"I know how to tell if it's alive," Nan said, and she picked off a flaky piece of bark. Underneath, the wood was dusty brown, and a small shiny beetle scurried away.

"Oh," Nan said, and she ran to look at the little tree.

18

WHEN A TREE IS DEAD, LOTS OF INSECTS LIKE TO EAT ITS WOOD.

"Oh!" she said again, but in quite a different way.

"Look!"

Underneath the shrivelled remains of one of the flowers was a tiny swelling.

"Will it grow into an apple?" she asked.

"I think it might," I said.

YOU CAN STILL SEE THE REMAINS OF THE FLOWER ON A FULLY GROWN APPLE.

We asked a man to come and look at our
big apple tree. He said it was very old,
and had a disease under the bark, and ought
to be taken away. Nan asked if the little tree
could catch the disease, but he said no,
it would be all right.

THE MOST COMMON DISEASES
APPLE TREES CATCH ARE SCAB,
CANKER, MILDEW, SILVER LEAF
AND BROWN ROT.

INSECTS ATTACK THEM,
TOO, AND GRUBS FEED
ON THE FRUIT.

It was a hot summer day when
the man came back to cut the big apple
tree down. The trunk was hollow, and
there were lots of insects living under the bark.

We piled up the branches by the hedge so
none of the insects had to look for a new home.

The garden looked very empty, and the sky
looked very bare. "The little apple tree will grow,
though," Nan said.

SOME APPLE TREES
CAN LIVE FOR AS
LONG AS PEOPLE –
EIGHTY OR NINETY
YEARS.

As the summer went on the little apple turned yellowish red. It swelled bigger and bigger until one day it fell off the branch when Nan touched it.

"OUR APPLE'S READY!" she shouted, and brought it into the kitchen. We cut it in half, and each took a bite. The skin was quite thin, and the apple was very, very juicy.

"It's sparkly inside," Nan said, and it was – sparkly white. "Maybe next year we can have sparkly apple pies."

"These are eating apples," I said. "They're not so good for cooking."

A NEW APPLE TREE MAY NOT GROW MANY APPLES IN ITS FIRST YEAR. MOST OF ITS STRENGTH GOES INTO GROWING WELL.

"Oh." Nan wiped the juice off her chin.
"But I like apple pies … and puddings."
She took another bite.

" I know, we can get another apple tree –
just like the big one."

And she hopped out through
the back door into the garden.

29

Index

*Look up the pages to find out
about all these apple-tree things.
Don't forget to look at both kinds
of words:* this kind *and*

THIS KIND.